CREATIVE

GENIUS

THE SAGELIKE AND MAJESTIC EXISTENCE

BY

COACHMAN AKEEM

TONY NDUBUISI IKEM

FIRST EDITION JULY 1998

SECOND EDITION. MARCH 2003.

THIRD EDITION JULY 2015

COPY RIGHT

COACHMAN AKEEM.

FOR INFORMATION WRITE COACHMAN AKEEM

OR Tony NDUBUISI IKEM

On <u>coachmanakeem@gmail.com</u>

Or <u>ikem.ndubuisi@gmail.com</u>

DEDICATED TO ALL FREE SPIRITS AND THE CAUSE OF TRUTH

AND TO THE FOLLOWING CREATORS IN MY LIFE.

MY HONOURABLE CHAIRMAN

CHUKA OKOSI. CHAIRMAN OF THE ROCKBOLT GROUP

MY LOVELY WIFE AND MY OWN LIFE COACH

JOYCE U. ONAIWU ESQ.

MY GENIUS SON AND THE REASON FOR MY BEING

CHISOM M. ONAIWU

MY LOVELY DAUGHTER AND INSPIRER OF MY VERVE AND DRIVE

JUBILEE A.ONAIWU

MY LIFESTYLE ENTRPRENEURIAL COACH AND SISTER

EVY IVY

MY PRESIDENT AT SHECHINAH BUSINESS SCHOOL AND CONSUMMATE SALESMAN

CHRRISTIAN UDOMSINACHI WOGU ESQ.

MY PARTNERS AT MULTIPRENEUR & KEEM LLP

DORIS EMEAHU ESQ. AND ONYINYE ODUNIYI ESQ.

(PUBLISHER OF EXPLORE MAGAZINE)

MY PARTNERS AT THE MULTIPRENEUR

TONY NDUBUISI-IKEM AND EDWIN URIRI, WHO BOTH

DAILY CREATE NEW FRONTIERS WITH ME.

MY SPIRITUAL MENTOR AND GUARDIAN

DR JOHN OKPARUGO WHO BELIEVED IN ME WHEN I HAD

LOST FAITH IN MYSELF

MY REVERED FRIEND AND ASSOCIATE

ATTAI EMMANUEL UDIA

CHIEF FRANK ONWUALU MY BELOVED MENTOR

LEKAN BABALOLA. A TRUE CREATIVE GENIUS

SINARI DARANIJO. MY TORMENTOR IN CHIEF

GREG ANOBILI WHO OPENED NEW WORLDS IN ME AND
PACKAGED ME FOR THE FUTURE. ALL GAVE ME THE
PLATFORM FOR MY SECOND SOJOURN AND
ACTUALIZATION OF MY OWN PECULIAR CRAZE OF 21ST
CENTURY GENIUS, CREATIVITY AND INNOVATION.

ACKNOWLEDEMENT

I wish to acknowledge the efforts of the following people who made this work possible.

The entire staff of the Franc Philemon Academy especially the following: Chuks, Emmanuel, Nonso Elliott, Chnedu Ohanu (Chii boy), and all the other beautiful people who have made me realize that the beautiful ones are now born. And thriving among us, regardless of the challenges and the obstacles they encounter daily in Nigeria.

My Partners at The Multipreneur Firm and Multipreneur and Keem LLP. Onyinye Oduniyi, Nnana Nkobi. Oritsema Eyeoyibo. Richmond Anyanwu, Gboyega Adeyanju, My beloved sister and adjunct professor at Illinois University, Springfield, IL. USA. Evelyn Ivy, Attai Emmanuel Udia,

Doris Emeahu esq. Felicity Orji.

My partners at Job Innovator.com and Que-Niche Hospitality and Tourism Academy Tony Ndubuisi Ikem. Edwin Uriri, Zanzi Moses Amechi, Sam Enemari

My inestimable Clients and Ogas at the top who put food on my table. Madam Elvira of E Bar, Lekki phase 1. Mrs Okoi MD of Spoilers Restaurasnt. Mr Eze GM of Brus View Hotel, Mr Ojukwu GM of Heavens Hotel and Suite

Argungi, Lekki. Mr Biodun Omolayo of Biodun Omolayo Art Galleries, 2nd Floor, City Mall, Onikan, Lagos.

My Mentors in the industry. Shina Eddo, Tayo Eddo, Mrs. Helen Eddo Ade Eddo Baba K Eddo and his lovely and industrious wife St. Bridget Eddo and the matriarch of the family Mama Eddo all of Cave Aficinado Night Club at 17 Joel Ogunaike st GRA, Ikeja, Lagos.

I acknowledge the genius of Toun Adeyanju aka Indian Princess an exotic dancer of incredible and renowned repute. My Pastor and General Overseer of Jubilee International Gospel Church.

Pastor Dr. John Okparugo and his revered wife Mrs Okparugo, My Pastor Joy. Pastors Christian and Chinelo Phillips of the House of Mercy who gave my life a divine and uplifting thumbs Up. Dr. Chris U. Marshall, Barrister

Chris Wogu Esq. President of the Schekinah Business School, Lagos.

My wonderful parents Mr and Mrs P.I.Onaiwu who gave birth to this process and nurtured the process. My lovely wife and children. Joyce, Chisom, Jubilee and Tory.

My beautiful neighbours at Oyadiran Estate, Mr Ulu, Mr. Chike, The Raro Edo Family, Olumide Afonja,   Mrs Franca Munis and NicK Munis. Without my big sister Franca I would not be alive to write this book. Dr. Ngozi Aikpopko and Family, Osagie Onaiwu and his lovely wife Nere and thelovely children. Uche Onaiwu, Dupe Munis and Ada George. Mrs Linda Issa Adejo (Princesh)

Thank you all for your inspiration and massive contribution to my life. I love you all.

PREFACE

We first published the Creative Genius at the North Western University Evanston IL USA in 1998.

The book was actually an accident for I did not plan it, but I had been doing an exhaustive research on what creativity was all about.

In this exhaustive process we stumbled on another powerful concept which was Genius and we realized that the two terms Creativity and Genius are virtually synonymous. Thus we had no choice but to merge the two concepts as one. The most important idea you will learn and grasp in this book is that the Creative Genius is an innate person, who looks within his own being for the solutions of his own problems or the creation of a new idea.

Every thing occurs twice in life. First and most importantly in the mental plane, before it occurs in the physical. We relocated from Evanston IL. USA because of the central theme of this book.

The Multipreneur Firm and Multipreneur and Keem LLP was established with only one goal in mind. "To inspire Nigerians look within our own Being for the simple solutions of many of our seemingly difficult problems. The Mulipreneur Firm is actually an incubator for creating geniuses.

We are and will continue to create geniuses out of Nigerians / Africans who give us the privilege to work with them.

The future of Nigeria is in the Nigerian. Nigeria is a sleeping giant waiting to be awakened to her own greatness and unlocking its great potential.

What we need are energizers in the geniuses who can midwife the process, give birth to it and nurture the life long process that will establish eternally our own peculiar brand of genius which we are currently utilizing in a negative manner.

The Nigerian Factor of mediocrity must be transformed into the Nigerian Factor of Creativity and Excellence. This is the only future we all possess.

Corruption in Nigeria will be greatly reduced when we start being creative. Indeed the environment presently is the one that kills true creative genius and exalts the mediocre and incompetent. We intend to reverse this process, we encourage you the beloved reader to take a more proactive stance for Nigeria and join us in doing this.

We have created an initiative to monitor the present government called; "Concerned Professionals Monitoring Change." www.CPMC.com.

You also have already taken the first step, you are reading this book, that means you have an affinity for genius as well. However go further and make your good better and your better best.

Look within your own Being Nigerian, discover your passion, master it and in the process become a Creative Genius yourself. This is what Self Actualization is all about.

Being a Creative Genius is the most powerful process of self actualization that is in very basic terms of you actualizing your own innate potential.

We believe in Nigeria and the Nigerian. Let us evolve from our present situation to higher levels of consciousness that can translate into a more humane lifestyle for us as a nation presently and in the future.

This is why we wrote this book Creative Genius and also adjusted it to the Nigerian situation. We invite you in joining us to become all we can be.

We can be reached online at;

www.The Multipreneur Firm.com.

www.MultipreneurandKeem.com.

www.University of Ideas.com

www.Franc Philemon Academy.com

www.CPMC.com.

www.Coachakeem.com.

E mail.

Ikeemagape@hotmail.com

www.Coachakeem2015@gmail.com

Telephone

0803-344-5756   0817-983-4018 0803-532-3508   0802-

648-6027

It is only that soul that has tasted of the good, bad and ugly facets of life, that can truly impact his or her fellow human beings for their highest good.

Shehu Mustafa Abdalah.

The simplest things in life are usually the most important.

True greatness may be found in the humblest places.

In the great battle of life, the most powerful weapons are wisdom and understanding.

Welcome to world beloved, congratulation for daring to buck the odds. You are about to learn what it takes to be super successful both in the Spiritual and natural realms.

I have a hunch you might be my kind of person, you want it all like me. Ha! Ha! Ha!. Don't we? Nothing Can stop us.

Super Success is a function of the heart than the brain, more of emotions than genetics and freedom than structure. The kind of drive that a hurricane uses to sweep away things it comes in contact with, so for the purposes of this chapter, please call me "Hurricane Coach" because I am about to devastate the world in a way it has never felt before. I just want you to stick around with me for the journey. It is not what we are but what we think we are that defines us. The more deluded we are in our dreams and fantasies, the more successful we can become. Great successes can be learned and my Soul is ready to soak it all up.

Success is about the life experiences and not genes, drive not education are the keys to achieving great success and power. Have you been through hell in life? Then stand up tall and proud you are on your way as from now to begin to experience your paradise, once you find your niche and master it. Genius is for those who have lived a roller coaster existence, not normal people with normal mediocre existence. It is for people who have been at the peak and bottom of life and can make sense of it and come out winners.

Winners never quit and quitters never win.

Now let us define who a genius is. A genius is a person who influences another for the good or bad, or who has an extra-ordinary intellectual power especially as manifested in creative ability or exceptional capacity or aptitude.

Creativity is defined as bringing something new into existence. So to merge the two as one. A Creative Genius is any person who influences another for the good or bad by bringing something new into existence which changes the world in a profound and fundamental way.

Beloved do you see that everything about you spells genius? You are a unique Being. Just by being who you are, makes you a genius.

You being in this world has changed the world. Don't you think it is left for you to take life seriously and carve out your own niche. I would like to have you as my neighbour in the exclusive residential area of Malibu Beach in Los Angeles, or if we don't like this scenario, we can hide in one of our deluxe villas in the Cozumel Island.

These are the traits that define genius and make them phenomenal people.

Vision

Dreams and Intuitive use of imagination

Tenacity

Persistence

Boldness

Consistency of purpose

Focus and concentration

Rebellious scourge of the establishment

Risk taking

Drive

Charisma

Self Esteem, Self Image, Self Confidence

Obsession with work

Passion and Enthusiasm

Beloved I want us to concentrate on reprogramming our subconscious. You know why people are different? I will tell you why.

All people are equal in the sight of God, but it is their consciousness, that makes them different or greater than their fellow human beings.

Consciousness not Circumstances rule great people.

As a Spirit Being, you have the innate tools of Consciousness in you. My job as your Life Coach is to teach you how to use it.

So let us re-program ourselves for great success, because no one can be free unless he is independent and makes his own income and control the use of his time.

So I shall define success as the ability to do what you want, when you want, where you want and how you want. You know why very few people can truly do this? It is because the most important gift that anybody can be blessed with is to control the use of his own time. Can you imagine going to play golf on a Monday morning, when everyone is going to work and doing what you do anytime of the day, because you can afford to. You do not have to be like the rest of the mediocre people in this world.

Think and act different. This is the essence of genius in our world.

Life is so funny, have you seen people, who try their best to be successful? They have three or more jobs, go to school at night / weekend, have a side income making more money for them, but they never seem to make it, because they seem to be fighting a losing war with the system. This is due to the fact that after they have paid their tax, rent and bills, they don't have much left, and they work so hard, and do not have a life, they might fall sick, and spend all the money they have saved on trying to regain their health.

Strive to make a life for yourself and not just to eke out a living from your existence.

All political, economic, social and religious systems in the world want you to eke out a living so they can control and manipulate you. Only your inner Spiritual system can define a life for you.

Get a life. Duh!!!

There is a story I heard when I was living in Tel Aviv, Israel about an African who worked 18 hours a days in two different jobs, he was very disciplined and saved a lot of money: $15,000 to be exact which he had hidden under his mattress. One day he came back from work, fell asleep and never woke up again. He was dead. You know why? He had stressed his physical faculties to the extreme.

Brain not Brawn is what actualizes great wealth for you.

Many who achieve great things in life are amazed at their own accomplishments. Eminent innovators, superstars, celebrities, entrepreneurs are usually so immersed in their own driven need to achieve that they are not aware of the amount of money, knowledge or power they have. The concept is paradoxical, the more it is desired, the harder it is to get.

Show me what a man does on Monday morning and I will tell you the type of person he is.

Power is a woman, the more you pursue her, the more she will run away from you.

The only way to obtain more power is to forget about power itself and use the will to pursue the principles of power. As long as you want power you cannot have it.

Very true, most people that want to be rich won't get rich, but it is those who want to be the very best of who they are and can be in life that would strike it rich.

You are rich, just as nature is rich. All you have to do is give birth to your own genius.

Be Natural. Flow your gifts from your innate Being to the outside world.

Nature is the mother of great success while innovation is the father. Merge the two together to birth your genius.

Beloved , isn't it funny that most people try too hard to achieve their dreams, but their intensity becomes counterproductive to the process. They are so focused on their goals that they are incapable of functioning in a way best suited for success. The royal road to success is relaxed   concentration,   because   concentrating excessively on anything in life is counterproductive to the objective. Fear brings about that which one is afraid of and makes it impossible for one to achieve what he wants. Try singing a song you know too well, if you try too hard you forget your lyrics, but once you relax, it flows and you sing excellently. That is why singers who are celebrities are those who are confident of their ability and are relaxed in their consciousness, thus bringing out the best in themselves. When you have a dream or a goal, keep it in the background of your mind , but don't get anxious and panicky over it. All you have to do is to work on the step by step procedures that will take you to your destination. The things we want from life are given to us when we least expect it, that is why we have to learn to try our best but yet take it easy.

In my life I think about it when it comes to sex. When I want to prove to my lover that I am an excellent lover, I perform miserably. But when I am relaxed and I want us to enjoy the companionship of being with each other, it is a delightful experience. When I start making love to her, each thrust counts for us and that is when we have a great sexual experience. It is when we are not trying to prove a point of superiority or inferiority that we enjoy ourselves most. If one thinks of the goal, there is a good chance he will not achieve it because his own mind gets in the way. The mind must be allowed to do its job of recording our intentions but when it is done, we must remove it so that action can now replace the thought process.

When you become the very best of who you are and what you do, all the good things of life will run after you all the days of your life.

God gave us our will power so that we could use it to overcome difficulties or obstacles that present itself to us in life.

We can create order out of chaos, when we look into our own beings and if you have not learned this, you need not be dismayed because no human quality is beyond change. So to achieve success, whatever weakness we have we will ferret it out, destroy it and build on our strengths. Very successful people are able to achieve greatness because they truly believe they deserve it. When you believe in yourself, your belief endows you with the attitude that grants you great power.

It is all a question of your belief system.

Instant power like instant gratification is an exercise in mental masturbation. Great power emanates from years of sweat and toil and cannot be attained overnight. It is the by product of enormous mental, emotional and physical struggle. True power comes from within. Knowledge as well as authoritarian and charismatic powers are merely the external manifestation of an indomitable belief system.

The greatest trees in the world do not grow overnight, it takes a long time for it to get there. The longer the duration, the more majestic the tree.

Great people are ordinary people who are obsessed and possessed with the drive of actualizing their own innate potentials. Such people are bred and born. Throughout the ages, there have been instances of people with few genetic gifts who attained power. The great learned to be great, they were not born with it. Beloved, doesn't that give you so much happiness that you can learn to be great as well?

Let us examine the lives of a few great souls in history. We shall start with Antar, who was born in AD 615, he was poet, soldier and great chivalrous figure of the East. The most renowned warrior among the Greeks was Achilles, the greatest poet Homer. Antar is the Achilles and Homer of the East combined. What Roland is to the French, Seigfried to the Germans, St George to the English is what Antar is to 335,000,000 souls of the Mohammedan world. In the literature of the East he is known as the "ABDUL FOUARIS" (The Father of Heroes). Gotteus (Arabic Philosopher AD 615 – 710) says that even in the cities of the Orient today the loungers over their cup can never weary of narrating the exploits of this great black son of the desert, who in his person unites the great virtues of his people, magnanimity and bravery with the gift of poetic speech.

Few started lower in life than Antar, few if any have risen higher in self esteem, and affection from those who despised them. He was born of a slave mother in the midst of the proudest of all peoples; the Bedouins, horsemen and plunderers of the desert.

Moreover Antar was extraordinarily ugly, he was flat nosed, bleary eyed, harsh features and had long drooping ears. He was also hair clipped and black. But his eyes! Ah from them flashed sparks of fire. His father wealthy Shaddad, chief of the Abs ignored him completely, while his mother hated him and sent him to mind cattle, to get him out of her sight. But like David of the scriptures, Antar was destined to flash into fame and fortune and become a massive legend in history.

From his infancy he gave proof of his extra-ordinary force and courage. By the brilliance of his act, he redeemed his extraction and won his freedom. Like most Arab chiefs, he was skilled in poetic art, as well in the use of sword. Deprived of the advantages of good looks and birth, he won merit by the force of his soul, by the power of his Spirit and the indomitable energy of his character occupying the foremost rank among men.

Let us also consider the life of Aesop, 560 B.C. Inspirer of the world's greatest minds. The influence of Aesop on Western thought and philosophy is profound. Plato,

Aristotle, Aristophanes, Solon, Cicero, Julius Caeser, Caxton, Shakespeare and other great thinkers found inspiration in his words of wisdom. Socrates spent his last days putting his fables into verse. The book that have been written about him and his works would fill an immense library. His writings have been translated into every language of the civilized world.

Aesop was a native of Phrygia in Asia Minor and a negro slave, flat nosed with lips thick and pendulous and his black skin gave him the name Aesop. But yet the wisdom of his mind shone through to make him one of the greatest souls in history.

It is not the circumstances of your birth, or the one that life puts you in that counts because that can be changed.

But it is the consciousness you attain for yourself and live by that determines your destiny.

The two successful people I have described were inspired to fulfil their internal images and fantasies and in so doing achieved enormous power and success. Really, talent is of little importance. There is nothing as common in this world as talented fools who make nothing of themselves and allow themselves to be restricted by their circumstances. For the super successful people, failure imprints and indomitable resolve to try harder and succeed.

Success can be defined as a series of failures and frustrations, held together by the strong strands of determination and persistence.

Examine the case of Malik who lived in Perlow (1548 – 1628) and was one of the most brilliant and military strategists of India. Though he started life as a slave, he rose to become an able man. In warfare, in command, in sound judgement, in administration, he had no equal. History records no other instance of an Abyssinian slave who rose to such eminence.

Moshood Kashimawo Abiola started life as a fire wood cutter and rose to become one of the most successful entrepreneurs in history in his time. His majesty King Sheheu Mustafa Abdalah failed repeatedly in business, but realized his dream of running a global business empire known as Agape Universal PLC. Nelson Mandela overcame twenty- seven years of incarceration to become the first black President of Independent Republic of South Africa. Tayo Solagbade resigned as a

Senior Manager in Guiness breweries to start his Self Development Academy and become an icon and pillar in the Management and Human Resource Industry of corporate Nigeria.

Carolyn Richards overcame the juvenile delinquency of her youth and with lots of drive, inspiration and strong convictions in God, she transformed herself into one of the greatest innovative speakers the world has ever known.

It is not so important the hand that we are dealt, but the desire and obsession with which we play the hand. Will and Drive are more important than all the talent in the world.

Goals have to be clarified, qualified and quantified in your subconscious reasoning before it can be actualized in physical reality. Carolyn Richards.

Nurture not nature is the fundamental basis for all genius and creativity.

Whatever you nurture grows, whatever you ignore dies.

Human Beings are not limited by the traits that they are born with. It doesn't primarily determine our behaviour, but what we learn and our environment especially what we actually experience and learn and our environment especially what we actually experience and learn as we grow, is what determines our destiny. Just as money begets more money, so does success beget more success. As we have stated earlier the great learned to be great. You must have the drive and passion to pursuing your dreams at all cost.

For you to be extremely successful, you must sacrifice anything and everything irrelevant in your life towards achieving your goals in life. You must be driven with the internalized desire to be the very best you can be in life. You must sacrifice the profane for the profound. You must be passion incarnate.

Anything that comes between you and your dreams must be destroyed. You should not even allow yourself to get in your own way but learn the art of soul mastery as well. You have to focus and condition your entire existence.

Spiritual

Mental

Emotional

Physical

Towards the realization of your dreams, anything short of this is self defeat. It is the complete immersion of your whole existence into your vision that creates it in reality. The body is electrified and powered by its source of energy. High energy emanates from the mind and not the body and it is often the by product of a driven personality. The lives of great people clearly demonstrates their abnormal drive, or that high energy is conducive to super achievement. Anyone interested in breaking rules to create his own reality and blaze new trails must have high energy.

High energy is the sunshine of your vision, just as electricity is the light of the bulb.

Great people are different from normal people because they are over achievers, unlike normal mediocre people who are under achievers. Great people are never normal as defined by societal standards. This is because geniuses demand that we break or destroy all existing values to create our own values.

Great people don't follow dogma, they create it.

As Carolyn Richards stated creative people apply the principle. The "U.N.I.T.Y principle which stands for:

U	Utilize
N	Natural
I	Intellectual
T	Talent
Y	Yourself

This is what makes them very successful because they apply this principle in their life.

Geniuses are a little bit eccentric. The difference between genius and insane schizophrenic people is how they channel their energy .While the former channel the energy towards a goal, the other is left to run riot. Geniuses must be obsessed and possessed by their dreams and thus be able to work with such energy that activates them towards their dreams.

Those who spend eight hours sleeping daily will be denied one third of their existence as well.

When normal people sleep, geniuses are working to create and make their dreams a reality. They do what others do not do, and get what others do not get.

Individuals with normal aspirations and goals typically achieve normal success and those with abnormal aspirations and goals typically achieve abnormal success. Normal people are the middle class strata of society, because they detest extreme. Their normal aspirations ensure normal success and guarantees they will avoid terrible failure but predestine them to mediocrity. That is why they are quick to criticise very successful people because they instinctively know they do not have what it takes to achieve such success.

It is impossible for the abnormal visionary to end up like this or where mediocrity resides because mediocrity cannot stand the very intense heat of high energy. The visionary either makes it very big in life pr becomes a miserable flop.

When you are a genius in the bud, people, might look down on you today, but they will definitely look up to you tomorrow. You will never see eye to eye with them.

Super success and impossible goals emanate from the impossible dreams of abnormal people. All great souls have a break the rules mentality. It follows that if I can drive myself relentlessly to achieve my goals, I can inspire anybody in the world as well, because in me are so many different kingdoms and the secret about life is to make sure these kingdoms in me are not warring against each other, but are at peace with each other and help me in achieving my dreams. For great souls it is not the physical achievement that counts but the emotional achievement. Most great souls are hypomanic. They are aggressive, assertive have a dare devil attitude, charismatic, omnipotent confidence and a great personality. These souls are always in an euphoric state created by their intense desire to see their vision come to pass. The most creative people in the world have been people who had very poor formal education.

It is indeed a miracle of nature that modern formal education has not stifled the holy curiosity of the mind. Albert Einstein.

Intelligence as seen in knowledge can be counterproductive to great success in virtually all fields of life. Life requires focus on action and not thinking. This is what formal education is all about. Graduating from a good school with a good degree predisposes you to start from the middle and not the lower trenches where all true creative geniuses begin. More often than not people with great potential, who know they are not well educated tend to give their best to life, because they know if they do not they will starve.

Be that as it may, anything that you do from the heart and soul invariably becomes very successful. That is why such people who know themselves normally have the last laugh. I make bold to say that among the middle class, the Ibo people in Nigeria do not have a lot of formal education, but yet they are richer than their Yoruba counterparts who have all the education.

They have life's most important degree which is: "Qualified by Experience." (Q.B.E)

Success is based on will and drive to achieve your vision, and not mere mental or intellectual capacity.

Intellectual capacity like religion is the very antithesis of genius and creativity. It is better to be educated and graduate in the school of life than any other school created by man's thoughts.

Man's thoughts are restricting and confusing but nature's thought are simple and liberating.

Knowledge of life provides the tree of life which bears the treasures of life as its fruits.

Life is knowledge. If only you know how to tap into it. It is this kind of knowledge that produces phenomenal success, whatever field you are involved in.

For you to live a sage like existence in life, knowledge and truth must be your God.

Most people's God is very abstract, your God must be as real as your life. For it is in this knowledge you become divine.

You must revere and worship knowledge and use this wisdom to attain the peak of success.

Great souls are described as self made because they are self taught.

All true greatness and success comes from within.

You must know where you are going and why and then proceed with enthusiasm and passion. Heuristic learning must be your teacher and you must try and fail and keep trying, till you establish great success for yourself. To quit on the road to success is to give up your right to live.

We must fail forward to success.

A self taught person has more knowledge and wisdom than all the graduates taught in the best schools in the world. You must also believe in life to keep you safe, protect and watch over you. This   is what makes you confident of the unknown and content with high risks environment, because you know God who began a good job in your life will always finish it . It is very helpful to have fantasy mentors or heroes that inspire us. As we emulate them to become the very best.

Myths are clues to the spiritual potential in human life.

He wrote in HEROES. "All of life's potential are innately unconscious, because genius derive sits vision from unconscious vision. That is why you will discover that most great people have a passion for learning.

Books are to genius what water is to the fish.

Imagination does create its own reality, for it is in the mind of man that all of possibilities exist, waiting to be manifested. It is because of my love for life and books I knew I was going to be an unprecedented success, spiritually and materially that would change the course of history for ever. That is why when we have internal visions, they become self fulfilling prophecies, which actually comes to pass in the material realm. Thus it is important in choosing our role models in life, the more impossible it seems our heroes are, the more impossible and grand will be our achievements. Reality or fantasy makes no difference because there is no such thing as reality. All of life is an illusion.

In the cosmic mind if the reality of your being and the fiction of your dreams can merge together as one to create your actual reality, then you are a genius.

Beloved if you want to be successful you must learn to risk and fail without remorse. Geniuses are rebels with a cause. They go where others fear to tread and are rewarded for this particular form of boldness. They see the world through childlike imagination and have an all things are possible mentality, building castles in the sky, which simply means abnormal dreams which others deem to be impossible to fulfil. Human life is ruled by and molded by the subconscious against the active will. Reason and logic are the faithful servants of willpower.

All behaviour is unconsciously driven.

All forms of behaviour both creative and otherwise originate from the unconscious. A few souls become great because they learn to draw from their inner well of great treasures. Creative people manifest what they already know to be true in their consciousness. It is the unconscious that fuels the energy of our physical apparatus which drives us to great achievements.

Genius is the process of rising from grass to grace.

It is intense participation in our vision that creates our drive: self image, self esteem, and self confidence. As Nancy Pier stated, "The most creative people seem to be the ones with the easiest access to the unconscious."

Imagination is the foundation of genius and creativity.

A mind that has nothing to lose has already given his all to life, all that remains for such a mind is to receive from life. It is desperate people who create their own reality because they do not look for reasons they will not succeed. But actually on the contrary believed they have succeeded, no matter how improbable this might be.

Geniuses are souls who have learned to play God by calling those things that are not as if they are.

Be that as it may, the road to success becomes easier to travel, when one has been in the pits of life, the journey of life becomes more clearly defined and self motivation takes over. With mortality on the line great risks take on a different perspective, the journey becomes less painful, when there is little to lose and much to gain. People who are secure in what life has given them are very reluctant to risk everything because they have much to lose. This applies to spirituality as well and this is what Jesus meant when he said: "It is easier for the camel to pass through the eye of a needle than the rich man to enter the kingdom of God. " This is so because the rich man's soul is already satiated with the things of the world.

To continue from where we stated earlier, risk taking is directly proportional to the need one intends to   in the subconscious reasoning. It is really more mental than physical. Someone who is very thirsty will do anything for a drink of water, more so than someone who is not thirsty. It is the internal need that creates the superman persona of the genius.

Great pain and stress can lead to discovery and put the laws of creativity in one's inner being into action.

The black slaves in America, because they were completely brutalized by their white savage oppressors created jazz, blues and soul music to soothe their pain. Now this is the very foundation and core of American music today. That is why African Americans today must seek consolation in the fact that whatever they are going through will in time bring out the best in them, if they choose to be inspired by it. Life emerges out of chaos not despite it. Nobody succeeds in a big way except by risking failure. For we mount to heaven mostly on the ruins of our cherished schemes finding our failures were successes. Our highest hopes are often dashed to prepare us for better things. The failure of the caterpillar is the birth of the butterfly. The passing of the bud is the becoming of the rose. The death or destruction of the seed is the prelude to its resurrection as the plant. It is in the night, in the darkest hours, those preceding dawn that the plants grow best and increase in size.

When we begin to not take our failures seriously, it means we are ceasing to be afraid of them. It is of immense importance we learn to laugh at ourselves.

Defeat is a school in which truth grows strong.

Do not brood over failures, defeats and mistakes, it only weakens your will. Just reflect a while on why you have failed in the first attempt and try to be careful in the second attempt. There is no failure except when one stops. There is no defeat except your own inherent weakness of purpose. Even after the greatest defeat, the depressing thought of being a failure is best combated by taking stock of all your achievements. If you can learn to learn from failure, you can pretty much go anywhere you want to go.

This is the main theme of my alma matter: King's College Lagos, when it states in its school song as follows: "If you fail look closely, seek the reason why, you are bound to conquer if you try."

Being defeated is often a temporal condition, giving up is what makes it permanent.

He who attempts to avoid all failures and misfortunes is trying to live in a fantasy world. The wise man realistically accepts failure as a part of life and builds a philosophy to meet them and make the best out of them. What then is defeat? Really nothing but education and the first step towards doing something better.

There is one failure in life that is possible and that is not to be true to what one knows.

It is defeat that turns bone to flint, flesh to muscle and makes men invincible.

Move from being invisible to becoming invincible.

Do not then be afraid of defeat, you are never so near to victory as when defeated in a good cause. The hammer shatters glass but forges steel, crises makes genius but destroys ordinary folks. Geniuses make as many mistakes as weak people, the difference is that they admit them and that is how they become geniuses.

There is an African proverb which states: "He who admires the great paves the way for his own greatness."

A child that washes his hand properly will dine with kings.

The reason that geniuses create is because they are very positive people. Most people are very negative by nature. The habit of focusing on the ills of life and ignoring the positive things leading to accomplishment is far too universal.

The road to wisdom and legendary existence is to err and err again but less and less again.

From error to error one discovers the entire truth. If you shut your door to all errors, truth will be shut out. Of course we all make mistakes, it is how we learn, we are all experiences in training. The sages do not consider not making a mistake a blessing, they believe that the virtue of man lies in his ability to correct his mistakes and make a new man of himself. The failure in a sense is the highway to success in so much as what is false leads to seek earnestly after what is true, and every fresh experience points out the error we shall carefully avoid.

It is very important to know that despite success attained in the material sphere that life is not an end in itself. Your goal is not restricted to the physical world in which your body is living. It goes beyond the world of appearances. It is the attainment of divine perfection which is the nature of absolute beauty, peace and joy.

Genius is God @ work in humans.

One of the strangest characteristic of genius is the power to light its own fire. A distinguished quality of introspective personality is that the creative person has easy access to his or her own inner world.

The depths by which you crash will prepare you for the heights to which you will ascend. Catastrophe is the manure for phenomenal success.

Great successes are born out of failures, calamities and frustrations and not on small successes.

You must be able to overcome tragedy to become the very best of what you do. Let us examine the life of such a person in history. Kafur the Magnificent died AD 967, eunuch, ex slave who became the Pharaoh of Egypt. No story ever told of hardships overcame the rise from the depths of degradation to the heights of power, excels or even equals that of Kafur Al-Ikshidi, the obstacles he overcame were so great, that his triumphs made that of Cinderella look common place.

First of all he was black and while blackness is not a major handicap in the Orient. In Kafur's case, it was also because he was an alien with an alien religion and an alien tongue. His very name Kafur was a product of scoffing and ridicule. It means camphor and was the equivalent to the nick name of snow ball for black man. He was also fat and ugly as a walrus and walked around like one with splay feet and fallen ankles. In his earlier days crowds of youngsters followed him down the street mocking him as he went. Furthermore Kafur was also not only a stranger to the advanced culture of Egypt, but he was also illiterate.

Truly these were obstacles enough to block aspirations to even the most common place career, but there was yet another and the worst of all. Kafur was a eunuch, destined for the harem at an early age. His virility had been extirpated by the surgeon's knife. But within Kafur their burned the eternal spirit of the chainless mind. He showed this when he was being driven in shame through the streets of Cairo for the first time chained to another slave. When the latter who was hungry and tired was passing a bakery, and saw the tempting display of food, he said his greatest wish was to work in that place and never have to feel hunger anymore. Kafur equally hungry said that nothing less than being master of this great city would ever satisfy him.

What you see is what you get.

Life does not give you what you deserve but what you demand.

Kafur was bought by the Prince of Egypt to entertain his harem and just when his future seemed promising. He got an infection which caused his dismissal from the court and he sank lower and lower until he became a street urchin. This was the hardest period of his life. However when he was cured the Sultan re-employed him. And from there like the famed Joseph in the Bible rose like phoenixes from the ashes of his defeats to become one of the greatest pharaohs that Egypt ever has. Hence his name Kafur the magnificent.

Beloved I hope that this inspires you to be all you can be despite any obstacles that you might be facing now.

Geniuses are never interested in the material rewards of their success. Perfection is their goal and ultimate legacy to humanity. Geniuses are inspired from their soul to give their best to life. The difference between successful people and mediocre people is how they handle failure.

It does not matter what happens to you in life. What matters is how you deal with it.

Great crisis can imprint an indomitable will to excel in genius or the loss of will in failure. In Chinese the word crisis is made up of two characters, one means danger and the other means opportunity. This is what Genius is all about. In many creative geniuses, the need for success overwhelms their total beings. All power emanates from within, the deepest reality you are aware of is the one from which you draw your power. We are only as weak as our greatest fears and repressions, our secret fears may allow us to delude others but we cannot delude ourselves.

Real power can only come from those with internal integrity.

And as Ram Dass stated; "Power is a stateof mind." As long as you want power, you cannot have it, the minute you do not want power, you have more than you ever dreamt possible. This is true for great wealth as well. The power of a leader is the ability to influence other people's thoughts and make it appear as if the thought originated from the follower.

Power is based on emotional and mental strength not physical strength.

The genesis of power is to realize how important you are to everything else, and how much of an impact you can make. True power emanates from the inner essence of our soul. Geniuses gain fame and fortune through their intransigent and indomitable will. They operate at the top of the power hierarchy were personal magnetism which is the foundation of passion can move mountains.

Passion moves mountains.

Passion is like a hurricane that obliterates everything in its path to get to its destination.

When there is a will there is a way.

When there is a why there is a how.

Those who are capable of strengthening their will into an omnipotent "Let there be" will always dominate the weaker and mediocre souls to rise to the peak of their professions in just the same manner the cream in a mug of coffee will always rise to the top. Those who lead and excel in this world will be the workaholic risk takers who have great self confidence, drive, intuition and an obsession with their dreams, gaols and visions.

Reason is an instrument of will to power and knowledge is subservient to will. All the knowledge in the world will not help you if you do not put it in practice. If this were not true the University professors who teach economics and finance will be the richest entrepreneurs in the world and most Christians would have been so much more powerful than Jesus and surpassed him in miraculous achievements.

Power can also be charismatic, the word charisma comes from the Greek meaning gift of Divine grace. Those having it are blessed with extra- ordinary or magnetic powers of persuasion. They are able to influence others to do their wills, such trail blazers exude passion which move mountains and completely stifles fear. It is difficult to persuade others or gain a following, unless you have a philosophical tenet or special message with universal appeal. Great charismatic leaders are destroyers of existing orders. They are rebels with a mission, out to create new dogma and never follow.

Charismatic geniuses have a special kind of mental energy called emanating from within which is called the gift of "PRESENCE." The Jews call it "Chutzpah." Nigerians call it "SWAG." Such powers emanate from an internal belief system that can be effectively communicated to a desperate people who need to receive the message. Charismatics are effective in motivating others to follow their dreams.

If you have to create energy to feel and use it, then do it, this is the basis of charisma.

People who take life too seriously and frown a lot as a result because of their consciousness and perception hardly achieve much from life. This is the tragedy of the poor and the overtly religious.

People who flirt with life enjoy life most. It is those with relaxed consciousness who get the most of life. This is the supreme virtue of the truly wealthy otherwise known as the "Thumbs Up" mentality. Pastor Christian and Chinelo Phillips of the House of Mercy.

If you love what you do then what you love will also love you. This is the secret of all great success. Chief Frank Onwualu.

Beloved, you have to be such a confident charismatic that it is difficult to imagine yourself in any negative light. You must not even give yourself the luxury of thinking you will fail. This should never be a possibility, your belief should translate every potential obstacle. Thinking positively does make it so, you must be the consummate optimist who looks for reason to do something and not why you cannot do it. You must have your own internally empowered belief system to realize your dreams and vision.

Adversity seen from a positive light can transform obstacle into opportunity for success and tragedy into a thrilling success.

Nigeria must adopt this principle stated above and learn to change their negative perception of themselves into an opportunity for personal growth and re-creation or risk extinction and obliterating their own name and heritage from the comity of nations. Coachman Akeem

Beloved, your charisma and confidence must arm you with an invincible godlike attitude that nothing can deter you from achieving your goals. You must have an awesome belief in your own vision which would enable you to reach your goals.

There is a limit to the development of the intellect but none of the heart.

Charisma means learning to move with the flow and take life's clues letting the universe take care of you. A true charismatic soul is one who uplifts, encourages and empowers other souls. We are defined by the way we treat ourselves and treat other people. Success is being honest not only in your work but in your life as well. We are responsible for ourselves. Charismatic geniuses are persuasive and blessed with the gift of gab, due to the fact that they present compelling arguments in communicating a belief system to another person.

Passion and enthusiasm are fundamental to effective communication and sales of a concept. The creative entrepreneur with an innovative personality has mastered this art. Such people belief and their belief fires up their enthusiasm to such a point that they cannot be denied.

Effective leadership requires persuasion not giving orders. Sinari Daranijo.

I will also attempt to describe charisma as an endowment that sets leaders apart from ordinary human beings, these leaders become supernatural, superhuman, and exceptional with powers not accessible to ordinary human beings. Charismatic is fundamental to entrepreneurship, management of change, strategic vision and innovation. Most charismatics have an aura of magnetism that inspires others to follow them blindly towards their vision of reality. They inspire an intense passion that motivates them to action, such leaders are critical to the innovative process. Subordinates have been shown to be more self assured, work longer hours, find their work more meaningful, experience greater trust in their leaders and have higher performance ratings than followers of non charismatics but effective leaders.

The secret of empire building is the ability to drive other people as you drive yourself daily to achieve stated objectives to consummate your goals. Chuka Okosi.

Charisma is innate in everyone and can be developed and learned. Leaders must work at being charismatic if they are to be more effective. The charismatic has a vision that is creative and unconventional. He is optimistic and inspired by it which is contagious and motivates follower.

Charismatic leaders are potential sources of enormous transformation for all. Many of the world's greatest leaders have been charismatic. They care, belief and are willing to risk everything for their dreams.

Let us examine the concept of will power:

Successful innovation is a feat not of intellect but of will. Joseph Schumpeter

I happen to believe that there is only one cardinal sin and that is mediocrity. Martha Graham.

Will is the master, intellect the servant, which in effect means a person with a strong will can acquire knowledge, money and force. Nietzche's concept of will to power which he proclaimed to be the highest achievement of the consummate man: "The overman or superman". In Thus Spake Zarathustra, Nietzche said that will to power is man's basic motive in life suggesting that it was pervasive in all things. He wrote that the only thing that men or women want is power and whatever is wanted for the sake of power could only come to the self possessed man, one who did not fear other men. He used Napoleon as an example of his hypothesis describing him as the synthesis of the inhuman and superman. He used Goethe as a model of the overman or the archtype of the worldly antithesis of God. He saw Goethe as a man who had organized the chaos of his passion, giving style to his character and becoming creative in the process.

Nietzche went on to emphasize the tremendous need for such great men in the world. He insisted that man must become a creator instead of remaining a mere creature as society has conditioned and programmed him.

Striving for perfection, superiority and power is fundamental to all humanity. Creative geniuses acquire power internally through the sheer force of their wills and take the power others have relinquished.

Power accedes to those who take it.

Such power emanates from within and not without. Those who attain great power are those who feel comfortable with complexity and ambiguity and they step forward to assume power. They have an indomitable belief system , that dominates all anxiety. True power lies in the source of power, not in life events itself, but from the supreme power of the universal cosmos. People who know where they are going will attract disciples, those who don't know are destined to become followers looking for knowledgeable leaders who have an invincible willpower.

Most importantly love is the greatest force that exists in the universe. The need to love and be loved is the most basic and primary human need that has ever been conceived. When we look at creation from this spiritual perspective, it is easy to find our niche in the world and bless others with it.

Will Power and Self Actualization

Many people are insecure and looking for leaders endowed with the conviction of their beliefs of their beliefs. People want to follow powerful leaders regardless of the price and if the destination be hell, so be it. Will power is greater than knowledge. Anyone striving for knowledge must use the power of the "will" over "self". Creative innovative and entrepreneurial ventures all demand leaders with strong wills. The foundation of creativity is actualizing one's potential.

The only powers that seldom are lost and never take place away are charisma and will. These are personal powers that emanate from within. Charisma instils attraction. Will instils psychic or libidinal energy.

Passion Incarnate

Passion breeds success! High energy can overcome many obstacles on the road to the top. As discussed earlier, it is the road to the top. As discussed earlier, it is the enormous success of creative geniuses. Their high energy was not inborn but learned. Their vital energy and drive were external manifestations of some inner force that they achieved at all costs. How did they develop such an omnipotent drive? Why are some people more active than others?

Great success is all about mental and emotional energy and not physical strength.

Creative Geniuses have an unrelenting need for work beyond economic need. It is stimulating not boring. Such is the mental influence of the hyperactive. Hypomanics are mentally and not physically driven. Their energy emanates from the inner essence of their soul which is their life force.

You must have the ability to generate your own insatiable energy from within. You become what you think. If you think fast you will act fast.

Will is the difference between success and failure, the genius and mediocre soul. Most people have not mastered the art of self motivation. You should learn to do this and energize yourself with introspection.

Happiness, good mental and physical health consists primarily of using one's ability to the fullest.. Creative people are happy only if they are free to create. Success will accrue to those who are willing to pursue their dreams whatever the cost. Beloved you must understand the value of concentration and make it an integral part of your life, if you are going to achieve great success.

The Royal Road of Concentration

Concentration is the "Royal Road" that leads to success.

It is not enough to dream, it is not enough to use your imagination to focus on how you will get there, But you must focus on your goal with an angelic intensity. You must concentrate all your mental and physical energies towards the attainment of your goal. You must select that one target and unleash all your fire power, everything in that one target and even if it is a volcanic mountain, it will shift oh yes!

The point is that nothing in life can be achieved without concentration, for all great people learn to focus absolutely, they learn to deploy an iron will, they learn to root out anything that is not relevant to the attainment of their dreams and goals, they learn to cut out all the nonsense and go for it.

Beloved the perseverance of hanging in the tussle when a tough problem is around is of utmost importance. The tendency to accept defeat will strongly resist this ousting process, but the problem must be attacked repeatedly with positive thought and faith as assuredly will give way if one has the will and fortitude never to give up. For they have not created the difficulty that can suppress a man who has the yeast to rise.

I find that in life most affairs that require serious handling are distasteful. For this reason I have often believed that the successful man has the hardest battle with himself rather than the other fellow. To bring one's self to a state of mind and the proper energy to accomplish things that require plain hard work is the one big battle that everyone has, When the battle is won for all time, then everything is easy.

The secret of success is the relentless pursuit of perfection.

It is not enough to begin, follow through is necessary, mere enrolment in a school will not make you a scholar. The pupil must continue in the school through the long course, until he has mastered every branch. Success depends on staying power, the reason for failure is lack of perseverance. Beloved do you have any goal you want to accomplish? Then you must press on. Nothing in this world can take the place of persistence.

Great souls who have attained things worthwhile in this world have worked while others idled, have persevered when others gave up in despair, have practised early in life the valuable habits of self denial / delayed gratification, industry and singleness of purpose. As a result they enjoy in later life, the success so often erroneously attributed to good luck. For it is one of the universal truths in life that the great high road of human welfare lies along the old high way of steadfast well doing and those who are persistent and work in the true spirit will invariably be successful.

Success treads on the heel of every right effort, The person with the average mentality but possessing control with a definite goal and a clear conception of how it can be gained and above all with the power of application and labour wins in the end. All the performances of human art which we admire with awe and reverence are examples of the relentless force of perseverance.

Beloved take heart, each day gives you a chance to start anew, to try again. Each night is a wall between today and the past, each morning is the open door to a new world, new vistas, new aims, new efforts.

There is a tide in the affairs of men which when taken at the flood leads to great fortune, if omitted all the voyages of life bound to end in shallows and miseries. The one who works need not be a problem to anybody, opportunities multiply as they are seized, they die when neglected. Life is long line of opportunities.

Do you know why people fail? I will give you one big reason, it is that they do not develop their greater abilities, greater sales strength, greater resourcefulness, because they do not optimize their abilities or opportunities. We do not need more strength or more ability or greater opportunity. What you need is to use what you have.

People fail greatly when all the time, they have in their possession the same assets that others are utilizing to accumulate a fortune. Life doesn't cheat, it doesn't pay in counterfeit coin, it doesn't lock up shop and go home when pay day comes. It pays every man what he has earned. The age old law that a man gets what he has earned hasn't been suspended. When we take this truth home and believe it, we have turned a big corner on the high road that runs to success. Beloved, nobody's problem is ideal.

Nobody has things the way he would like them. The thing to do is to make a success with what material you do have. It is a sheer waste of time and soul power to imagine what you would do if things were different, they are not different. The ladder of success is like a prostitute, it doesn't care who climbs it. Life js really learning to take the opportunities as it presents itself. If one doesn't learn to do this there will be very little chance of that person becoming great in life. The Creative Genius is a by product of his passion incarnate. He has a promethean temperament and sees the total picture in everything he does, not only does he see the tree he sees the forest as well . Such a great soul has an intuitive vision in everything he does, not only does he see the tree, he sees the forest as well, he has an intuitive vision of his adversary's every move before they implement their plan. He fights every battle in his head before he fights in the field. He views life as a game planning all the moves he makes in it like he would in a chess game. He has an omniscient vision of how the game should be played and uses duplicity and the unexpected to win. In business he is a master of surprise shocking everyone in making the most unexpected moves. He blazes new trail and never follows convention. To him speed is king and he must move so much faster than the competition, to achieve his goals. Only someone with total confidence and intuitive vision can move swiftly in any profession. He believes completely in his own ability, thus his belief translates into speech and ability to lead. He considers himself to be like Jesus that is: "He is the way, the truth and the light." This makes him very charismatic which attracts people to him, who will help him carry out his vision. Most people never win because they are indecisive and lack confidence in their actions which causes them to hesitate until the opportunity is lost. The genius's supreme confidence comes from the holistic knowledge of where he is going. A genius must be incurably optimistic and be a dealer in hope. She always expects to win and therefore does , and her positive attitude, swift action leads to her great success and causes her to believe she is invincible. Such a genius is often driven by delusions of grandeur that inspire her to superhuman achievement.

Enthusiasm, wisdom and passion are the secrets of a genius's greatness.

The creative genius is a principle not a personality. As was stated earlier, these are the people that are responsible for the world's civilization.

Geniuses are the true minority on earth.

"The man who produces an idea in any field of rational endeavour, the man who discovers new knowledge is the permanent benefactor of humanity, In proportion to the mental energy he spent, the man who creates a new invention receives but a small percentage of his value in terms of his material payment, no matter what fortune he makes, no matter what millions he earns." From Ayn Rand in ATLAS SHRUGGED.

Genius gives more to life and so is entitled to take more from life.

The creative genius is a soul who asks why of the universe and let's nothing stand before the answer to his mind. The Creative Genius is a voracious reader and loner and views life from a philosophical and metaphysical perspective. He has an emotional and internalized belief in his own omnipotent destiny, thus power and influence never trail far behind the imprint of greatness, for it is his destiny and soul conviction that makes him change the whole world.

It has been said that there are seven great wonders of the world, if this is so, you are the first of the wonders, because you beloved, are the greatest miracle that ever existed.

The creative genius is a soul who knows, such a one has the revelation of the inner voice and operates from his own internalized view of the world. The genius is a rebel who values nonconformity in all things. His creations emanate from his own imaginative fantasies. He violates social decorum to the chagrin of the whole society and is never constrained by what was and therefore is able to create what could be. The only authority that a genius gives credence to is a super being known as himself. They are wild birds that must stay free and never be confined in the confined in the cages of society. Innovation is his forte. He is more interested in destroying the existing order to be innovative in a new way.

Never attempt to resolve a design or solve a problem, until the idea has taken a clear shape in your imagination.

Work should be the creative and joyful essence of life.

All innovations receive its power from the life force and both man and his creations are identical and in a state of becoming.

Crisis is the catalyst for the genius's greatness.

It was Helen Keller who stated that: "Courage is the price that life exacts for granting us being."

Geniuses never protect the status quo, they envision a greater future and destroy the present to create the new status which is the process of creative destruction.

The genius is the rubicon of extroversion and introversion, he is energized by the external world of opportunities but also delights in the internal world of soul analysis. For such a soul he is always at war with life, always fighting to survive, risking everything, putting all his cards on the table.

The greatest risk is not doing nothing. You will never get into trouble if you never do anything, but you will never get anywhere either. A faint heart never wooed a fair lady.

It is only by risking our persons from hour to hour that we live at all and often our faith before hand in an uncertified result is the only thing that makes the result come true.

Lead, follow or get out of the way. Never get discouraged and never quit, because if you never quit you are never beaten.

The "AS IF" Principle

Peak performance athletes and overachievers are visualizers who see it, feel it, experience it, before they do it. Thinking makes it so. Psychologists tell us to dress the "role" or "image" of the job desired and the job will be ours simply because we fit the image or "identity" of that role.

Intuitive people prefer the abstract to the rational, insight to hindsight, quality to quantity, holistic to linear, macro to micro, sixth sense to common sense, long term to short term. Hunches to hard data, analogue to digital and future to past. These patterns and visions of reality allow us to explore the abstract and unknown. It is a prerequisite for creative thought and large scale innovation.

Intuition is not genetic but a learned ability. It is acquired by programming and imprinting and this lack of skill is based on societal conditioning and can be changed.

As Carl Jung stated; "The extroverted intuitive personality is uncommonly important both economically and culturally. He can render exceptional exceptional service as an initiator or promoter of new enterprises, he brings vision to life, presents it convincingly and dramatic fire embodies it.

The true genius experiences failure after failure until he succeeds through persistence. These failures drive them and becomes the catalyst to achieve great things, where a lesser temperament will give up to failure.

You have to believe in the impossible

The visionary's riches and wealth are the hints and clues that life gives him. But if the hints are not to be squandered the entrepreneur must trust his intuition. If you open yourself up, wisdom will flow in. Nobody can stop the Creative Genius from becoming a success, because the genius refuses to be discouraged. Imagination is his forte and acceptance by others never a factor.

Self confidence is mental and the first requisite to great undertakings. Sun Tzu stated this aphorism so well when he stated as follows: "Victorious warriors win first then go to war, while defeated warriors go to war and seek to win." Winning first occurs in the mind then in the field of battle.

Self image is the reputation we acquire with ourselves.

He was espousing the belief that self image is not what others think of us but what we think of ourselves. Great souls exude supreme self confidence which allows them to perform herculean tasks. This mental strength is what allows them to confront the many obstacles on their way to the top. As money breeds more money so does success breed more success.

They are anti authority and look to their own being to validate themselves, they question challenges or defy traditions their peers take for granted. Those with a feeling of great self worth are capable of exercising their creative energies , they destroy the present to create the future. Visionaries have a resilient self esteem, which is a vital trait needed to climb to the top, they are armed with an invincible self image and self confidence.

To achieve success one must think big. To change self esteem and self image it is necessary to start with self confidence an never allow a negative thought to enter into our lives. No one can think positively and negative at the same time, just as a river with fresh water cannot overflow with unclean water. Therefore it is logical to conclude that if one thinks about only positive things, there will be no room for the negative. Geniuses operate in an almost continual positive state of self confidence.

Those who are destroyed when rejected will never enjoy great success in life.

No one can be free unless he is independent. And indeed I may add that you can't be free without financial independence in the 21st century.

Never be deterred by the difficult or the impossible.

All great souls believe that they have a destiny to fulfil.

Great souls express their souls because they are free Spirits, just as the free horse runs swifter than the one motivated by whip or carrot.

This is why wealthy men will always be wealthy because they are not motivated by the fear of job termination or the reward of salary. They implicitly love what they do thus creating wealth in the process.

Wealth is when your work becomes play and your play becomes work, you simply birth great riches in the process.

Love for what you do is the mother of wealth.

Trail blazing concepts are the foundation of great discoveries in life. Risk is the function of finding comfort in ambiguity. The Creative Genius loves the new and untried. It is what drives them because they intuitively know that great success in products or art or life is never accomplished without risking failure. This is the rule for all aspiring entrepreneurs, find out where the experts are and go elsewhere. Trail blazing concepts are usually found in the least likely places making it crucial to violate the norm, choose a different path, opt for a unique strategy or pursue the bizarre.

You must be willing to risk and fail. Your boldness takes you to the peak of your career. Boldness (Guts) is the basis for living a productive life. Those who try to eliminate all risks from their venture also eliminate all success that could come from such a venture. Risk must accompany any great venture but must also be managed. There is no gain without pain. No venture, No success. No stress No attainment.

You must break eggs to make omellete.

A heuristic trial and error experimentation is the only way to solve great problems. Such activity is fraught with risks, but confidence and success ensue from both wins and losses.

Experimentation is better than formal education.

For you to fully live is for you not to be afraid of death.

It doesn't matter that the whole world does not take you seriously. All that counts is that you take yourself seriously.

All truth goes through three stages.

1. It is ridiculed

2. It is radically opposed

3. After going through intense persecution, it is
   accepted.

Innovation will be resisted by the fickle public and therefore anyone attempting to bring about change, must be prepared for rejection and confrontation. This is why the genius is a loner. It is impossible to create anything new and great within the confines of society. Creative Destruction is the formula for success. Mystics, philosophers, geniuses often discover the essence of life before others that is why a genius demands non conformity.

Whoever wants to be a creator in good and evil must be an annihilator and break values. Thus the highest attainment is being creative. One must be prepared to destroy what exists in order to create. A new home cannot be built unless the old one is destroyed. A genius greatest talent is an internal need to creatively destroy the existing order of things. He does not allow the experts to determine the values system that comes from within.

You must have a break the rules mentality for you to succeed in life.

Innovation is the child that is named after a fertile imagination gives birth to a new concept.

Life is a dream, a spiritual vision where the inner force becomes the driving force of life. To live your life based on the truth you know is to live an excellent life. You know what, Beloved? How can you be creative if you do not exert yourself? Creativity as seen in genius does not come from a sudden inspiration invading an idle mind and idle hands but from the labour of a driven person. The future exists first in imagination, then in will and then in reality. We should use our imagination to create dreams then convert these dreams to will in order to have them realized. Impossible dreams turn into improbable success because the will deems it so.

Mind control occurs by focusing properly your mental energy.

Anything in life worth doing well can only be sacrificed through great sacrifice and pain. But this is a small price you pay for your own re-incarnation. Because you re-invent yourself to suit your own internal picture of you. This is when you begin to star in your own movie in life.

From now on you can use creative visuslization and imagination to create new concepts and ideas. To expand your consciousness is to enlarge your perception into actualizing a different reality more favourable for yourself.

Nothing in this world can stop an intransigent will activated with psychic energy.

Geniuses get their ideas and inspiration from everything. They are adventurous souls who deviate from established routes. You do not ask for power in life you take it and dare anyone to stop you. This is because combat is good for the soul, since it challenges it. When you understand that life is war then you can buck the odds. Only a persistent Spirit can overcome the continual crisis and detour encountered on the road to any goal. It is those with passionate drive ano d vital force that can achieve their goals in life.

To be a creative genius, you must learn to squeeze lemons into lemonade. This is the lemon of societal rejection into the lemonade of your own creation.

Seek to establish your own authority from within, what is given by others can be taken by them as well.

Nothing in life can be accomplished in a state of non action and negativity.

Don't be afraid to risk. High risk begets high rewards, because you may need to kiss at thousand frogs to find a Prince or Princess. The wizard of genius is within us all, but it must be understood, unleashed, controlled and motivated for success to ensue. When you permit genius to express, there will be no stopping you, because all behaviour is unconsciously driven. Believing in something and thinking positively does make it so. Without confidence no creativity can occur.

Lead and never follow the crowd. Even though you are on the right track, you will be trampled if you stay still.

That is why we cannot afford the luxury of a negative thought. The roles we live in our lives tend to be predicated in the movies played in our subconscious. And not the one played in our conscious mind. That does not mean that the conscious movie cannot be changed, but the movies being played are beyond our conscious control, until we take steps to rewrite the original scripts in cognitive reality our subconscious. Our subconscious mind is where the macro-image is stored and will determine our performance on every stage in life. The mind dictates all the major roles we play in life.

Believing in our ability to be a genius is critical to making it a reality. Whether we become a genius or drug addict is not based on some subconscious wish, but on this critical image or belief system. In other words our subconscious mind has stored in the internal tape the destinies of our lives.

It has nothing to do with the conscious desire to be this or that. The genius is only pre-conditioned to attain that position in the real world, but probably has believed it to be his destiny since very early in life. The schizophrenic insane also believes he is a genius, but this is a departure from cognitive reality. The drug addict would never envision himself in the exalted role of a genius and therefore would never accede to it. Unfortunately he has a negative image which conditions him to that role, very early in life. His subconscious image of himself is imprinted in his mind and can never see anything else, unless he can change that internal image, he will have difficulty rising above the gutter instinct and will be destined to live on the internal movie of himself. These images are indelibly imprinted until changed.

They cannot be changed by the conscious thought process that say: "I would like to be a genius." The only way to change our macro unconscious image of ourselves is to rewrite our internal script or identify who we are. Geniuses are programmed early to strive for greatness and have an internal belief system that identifies them with success.

Everyone who has under achieved in life is also living their own preconceived imprint for failure.

Think Big and you will be big. Think small and you will be small. Thinking is what reinforces the subconscious.

The quality of your thought determines the quality of your life.

Geniuses possess an inexhaustible spirit and energy that makes them great. Their personalities give credence that most people strive for superiority and perfection. For one to be creative, one must have role models to be creative, one must have role models whom to emulate for creativity because it is contagious. That is why the very rich stay that way because they live in the same environment, attend the same schools and clubs and do the same things. This in an opposite manner is why the middle class stay that way and the poor stay very poor as well.

This is why you my beloved, must seek the knowledge to make you great and successful and it is not attained by acquiring a piece of paper. It is normally acquired by starting all the way from the bottom of your dreams and imagination to reach the peak of your career. Most geniuses are streetwise and have an uncanny knack for following their own gut instincts. This might make the path they have chosen in life more difficult, but it is also the most rewarding path. We must actually be willing to put our ideas into practice before we can create. Discovery is not intention. It is more or less the nature of an accident. Learning comes from doing and not just talking.

Perspiration not inspiration is the key to great success. One hundred hours weekly is rule not the exception. Anybody who ascribes success to luck has never achieved anything and has no inkling of the relentless effort which achievement requires.

Having an open mind is very essential to creativity, just as a closed mind is the very antithesis of creativity.

Reinvent yourself and turn your back against negative thought and superimpose your own values in the world.

Geniuses feel with their soul more than they think, that is why they can be passionate and filled with the zest of life and high energy to create what they want. It enables them to have larger than life fantasies that drive their creativity to maintain a utopian existence. It allows them to tap into their subconscious for the life they desire and in the process become immensely successful. Society should never castigate or begrudge geniuses their great success (even though they do) for you cannot strengthen the weak by weakening the strong. You cannot help the poor by destroying the rich. You cannot help human beings permanently by doing for them what they should do for themselves.

If someone becomes successful because they exerted themselves and possessed the guts and courage to follow through on their soul convictions, then they fully deserve whatever they have been blessed with.

Chart your course and follow it with integrity and success ensues.

Geniuses adhere to completion instead of procrastination or equivocation as ordinary people do.

They seek the principle in all they do and never yield to weakness because they understand the nature of society as a bully who has no respect for the weak masses but uses them and destroys them. The only way to stop a bully is not to become weak. Beloved, it is important to first sort out what you believe in, then apply it. Never compromise on this point. Successful innovation is not a feat of intellect but of will. Never let your mistakes deter or distract you, but learn from them and move forward in a positive way. Focus on the possibilities and not the process. Make the most of every opportunity, work diligently at what you do and be loving and passionate about it. This is what ensures great success in life., thus one must have great foresight in the art of seeing things invisible, for there is a limit to the development of the intellect but none to the heart.

It is people with impossible dreams who have the greatest chance to achieve impossible fame and fortune.

When you do not have excess knowledge, you know just enough. That is okay, because you have eliminated your ego in the pursuit of your life goals. With the ego removed, talent can take over to lead the individual towards success. Allowing your intuition to take over increases the chances for success in most ventures in life.

Be careful of your dreams, you might just wake up and find yourself there. Mark Twain.

Creative Genius tend to be spiritual by nature, but they must never devolve into religion, because this will inhibit there will to achieve their goals in life.

Spirituality enhances a great soul's world view but religion restricts it. The former is an expander while the latter is a constrainer.

Great souls / geniuses can be described as mythological in a sense, since they envision themselves as omnipotent beings. Their internalized images are epic and heroic. They seem to innately know their destinies, and believe in their fate to reach the top, so they never question their divine right to the throne. These dreams become their conscious realities, which were ultimately transferred into inestimable self esteem. It is this extra-ordinary self esteem that inspires geniuses to become great leaders, heroes and visionaries. Their unconscious need to achieve leads them to unprecedented heights.

Be overcome by your own self belief. Even when you know you are practising a kind of self deception. Act like a King and you are likely to be treated as one. Law 34 Strategy of the Crown. 48 Laws of Power by Robert Greene.

Most people are mediocre because they have a lack of self confidence in their own God given ability. They don't believe in themselves.

Creative Geniuses dance to their own tune and their own inner dreams.

Adversity a stumbling block for ordinary people is a stepping stone for geniuses which further motivates them to achieve their goals.

The nature of genius is to celebrate existence by actualising innate potentials and recognize that if they must succeed, they must do so by their own efforts. Never do they sit back and wait for miracles to save them, rather they make miracles happen by believing in the impossible and exerting themselves to the utmost. Excerpt from Genesis of Genius by Shehu Mustafa Abdalah.

Geniuses and other great souls adore knowledge and revere it above all things, they live by a philosopher that is fundamental to their success and power. It is apparent that all persons who are ambitious and want to achieve great success must have a distinct clear cut philosophy of life, that is the kind of mission statements that companies have. Without this it would be impossible to achieve success. You must live, fight and die for your convictions.

Step out of the surging crowd and make yourself a master.

In life it is what we know that kills us more than the unknown. It is the family and friends we know that do us the most harm, than the enemies who do not know so well. Often we are own worst enemies, since we know what our limitations are. Ignore your own internal self talk, and function at the peak productivity of your optimistic euphoria.. Have the mentality of a bumble bee who is supposed to be too heavy to fly, but doesn't know this and flies anyway. Beloved not knowing where to go to explore your truth is far more important than having a map, since the map is somebody else's perception of reality and it only outlines where somebody else has been. In order to go to where no one else has been, it is important to throw away the expert's maps and create your own. You must have a relaxed state of mind to ensure creativity. Successful geniuses are a combination of various traits, masculine and feminine, the most creative a hybrid of conflicting characteristics which creates a paradoxical balance of polarities. Competitive and compassionate, goal oriented and nurturing, intuitive and risk taking, amoral but possessing positive core values.

Be that as it may, one dimensional males and females are doomed to failure. One must persevere in life and have tenacity as well. Perseverance and persistence are crucial to the creative process.

A positive mentality or optimism is more important than physical skills. Most people have too much negative knowledge inhibiting their ability to perform. You must learn not to give emphasis to failures. You must believe to such an extent that your belief overcomes every potential problem. This is the reason why mad passion or passionate madness is the reason psychotic personalities are often creative and why their productions are perfectly sane. Most people get what they really want and become what they perceive themselves to be. That is why most geniuses have an all or nothing mentality, (aut nil) or my way or the highway kind of mentality.

Normal people do normal things and thus are not creative. Only the abnormal who dare to be all they can be are creative.

Think outside the box, that is where creativity and greatness abides.

Most people focus their lives on transient and illusory things. But geniuses focus on the core value of life that gives life its meaning and expression.

Intuition is the gift of the gods and logic its faithful servant. Albert Einstein.

I have long been in revolt from all things, from the authority of others, from the instruction of others, from the knowledge of others. I would not accept anything as truth, until I found the truth myself. I never opposed the ideas of others, but I would not accept their authority, their theory of life, until I had experienced it myself. J. Krishnamurti.

Creative Geniuses have a highly refined philosophy of life and live by it. I believe that every human being , no matter the education, social status or poverty, wealth, age, sex, political or religious belief system possess a special soul urge. The spiritual creative thinking is to challenge traditional thinking and go beyond boundaries. This does not mean being bizarre or freakish, which is mere foolishness and has nothing to do with the advancement of thoughts and accomplishments. But a soul urge to look at life's skyline and see beyond them to some new place, principle or realization, which constitutes a true advantage of the higher self over the lower self. It seems to go beyond boundaries. It is one of the principles of incarnation.

Surely we are not directed to earth life to re-invent the wheel over and over again. We are here to improve the past as human beings both collectively and personally.

Boundaries are to be exceeded. Boundaries are created to keep persons or things in or out in order to protect them from harm. But the greatest challenge they serve is to challenge human creativity, goal setting, aspiration and other positive endeavours. In fact there is no boundary to the positive human expression, except the one we create ourselves.

Now let us look at the beyond-the-boundaries type of person to see whether or not you fit that category, which most consider a unique niche in human family. What are the characteristics of a beyond boundaries type of person?

There are five of them.

First they like novelty, they are intrigued by the unusual and uncommon. They don't desperately try and fit in like the crowd. They are their own unique selves.

Next they are curious, they want to know what make things tick, they the who, what, why, where and when askers, those who turn over the stone to see that is underneath.

Thirdly they are tolerant, they tolerate others unusual thinking or behaviours, they are not bothered with the fact that other people's thinking differs from their own.

Fourth they are undismayed by chaos and hard work , Chaos is an opportunity to accomplish.

Finally they are risk takers, but not foolishly so. They do however balance logic and intuition, and if their experience indicates a favourable outcome, they go for it, often they fail but failure is a preliminary to success.

As human beings we are all born with extra-ordinary talents, we see ourselves as ordinary, we are all judgemental. We analyse ourselves with unwarranted modesty which has been crammed into us from childhood. We find it especially to break through that boundary, we compare ourselves to rare personalities who often without justification have leaped into the lime light. We judge ourselves by other standards real or imagined. Be that as it may, we must seek consolation in the fact that we are creative. We generate ideas, we originate aspirations whether they spring from a normal consciousness or higher level. We are capable of optimism and enthusiasm, and on the occasions that these qualities seem to be denied, we can produce them again and again for the same or other purposes. When we go beyond boundaries of ourselves, we become more than ourselves. Remember boundaries are to be exceeded and you can do it.

Start promoting yourself by learning and make yourself ready for new challenges. This is the mystical process of reinventing yourself into a new reincarnation.

You know what beloved? Most successful people started as failures but once they changed their minds they never looked back. What you put out is what you get back. What you put out is what you get back and the reason why so many people never get anything from life is because they put little or nothing out.